Copyright © 2000 by Nord–Süd Verlag AG, Gossau Zürich, Switzerland.
First published in Switzerland under the title *Zauberspuk bei Merrilu*.
English translation copyright © 2000 by North–South Books Inc.

First published in the United States, Great Britain, Canada,
Australia, and New Zealand in 2000 by North–South Books,
An imprint of Nord–Süd Verlag AG, Gossau Zürich, Switzerland.

Library of Congress Cataloging–in–Publication Data is available.
A CIP catalogue record for this book is available from The British Library.
ISBN 0–7358–1190–3 (trade binding)
1 3 5 7 9 TB 10 8 6 4 2
ISBN 0–7358–1191–1 (library binding)
1 3 5 7 9 LB 10 8 6 4 2
Printed in Belgium

For more information about our books, and the authors and artists
who create them, visit our web site: www.northsouth.com

Meredith's
Mixed-Up Magic

By Dorothea Lachner
Illustrated by Christa Unzner

Translated by J. Alison James

North-South Books
New York · London

A puff of smoke curled over the witch's house, tickling the tips of the trees. From inside came the sounds of clanging pots and clattering pans, and merry, cheery singing. It was the young witch, Meredith, making her breakfast. She was in a good mood. "Pop on the water, too-doodle-lee, milk for the cat, dee-dilly-dum, pour out the tea, too-doodle-lee, butter for the bread, dee-dilly-dum." Unfortunately, she took more care with the teapot than she did with the words of her peculiar song: "Dum-dilly dee-dingle come-dum bungle-dum!"

Suddenly Meredith froze in her tracks.
With her careless singing, she had spoken
the magic spell for uninvited guests!
Meredith didn't move, but the teacup kept
clattering. The cat hissed and disappeared
under the bed. A gust of wind whacked
open the door. Meredith ran to shut it, but
too late. *Swish!* Someone blew through the
door. *Plop!* He was already sitting at the
table, ready to eat. It was the little sorcerer.
"Hungry!" he screeched, and he pounded
his hands and feet on the table.

I can handle this little guy,
thought Meredith. I'll give him his
breakfast and send him on his way.
She served him bread and jam, herb
tea, and woodruff cakes. The little
sorcerer ate and drank and grew.
"More! More! More! More!" he howled.
So Meredith gave him sardines and
beans and the ham she was going
to have for supper. Munch, munch,
he ate his lunch, and with each bite
the sorcerer grew taller and fatter.
Soon he began to eat his way
through all the food Meredith
had stored in her pantry.

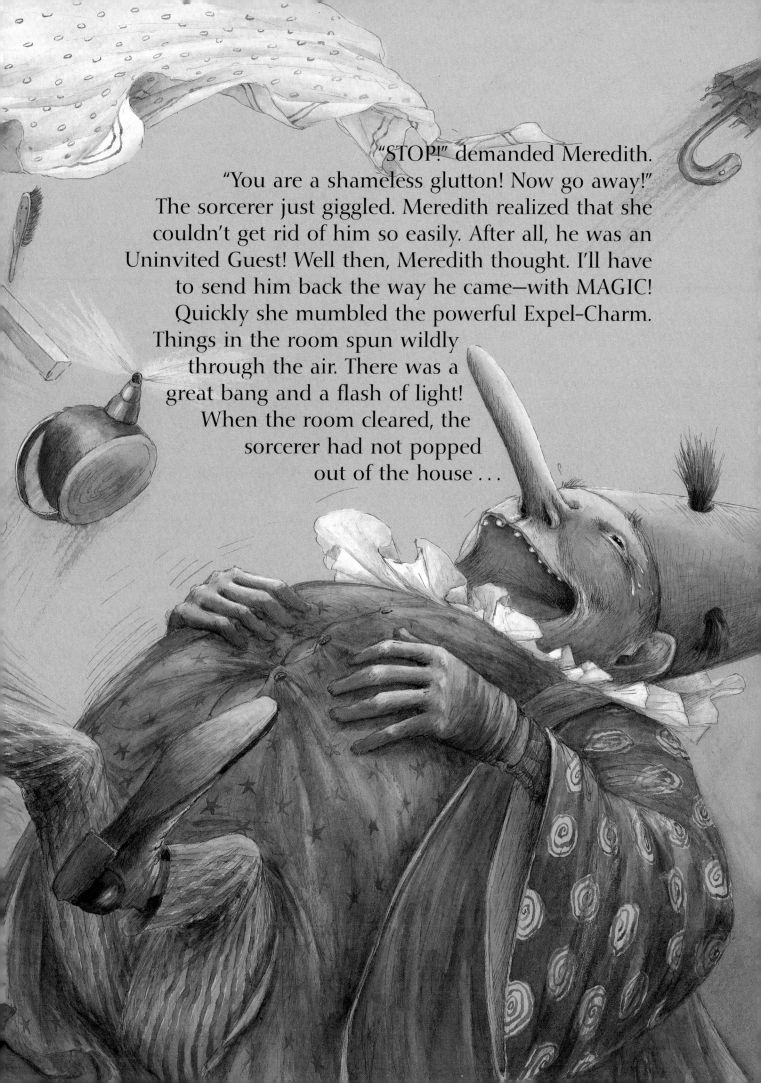

"STOP!" demanded Meredith.
"You are a shameless glutton! Now go away!"
The sorcerer just giggled. Meredith realized that she
couldn't get rid of him so easily. After all, he was an
Uninvited Guest! Well then, Meredith thought. I'll have
to send him back the way he came—with MAGIC!
Quickly she mumbled the powerful Expel-Charm.
Things in the room spun wildly
through the air. There was a
great bang and a flash of light!
When the room cleared, the
sorcerer had not popped
out of the house . . .

only a little bit into the air. He landed with a plop
on the coatrack.
The sorcerer was shocked.
And he was furious!
He decided to take revenge. With a sinister, secretly
whispered spell, he shrunk Meredith to the size
of his shoe. Even her hat had been shrunk. She
plopped it on and declared angrily, "You just wait!
See how you feel when you are covered in pond
slime from top to bottom!" She chanted a spell, and
the sorcerer became . . .

slime green.
He was shocked.
And he was furious!
He decided to take revenge. With a sinister, angrily whispered spell, he turned tiny Meredith purple from top to toe.
Meredith was so angry, her purple turned a shade darker. She would turn the sorcerer into a feather so that the wind would take him far, far away! In an angry rush, she squeaked out the words. The sorcerer disappeared, and in his place was not just a feather . . .

but a whole owl full of feathers! An owl with
a sorcerer's hat.
The sorcerer was shocked.
And he was furious!
He decided to take revenge. With a ringing
SHOO–WHOO, he turned Meredith into a toad.
Meredith the toad glared at the sorcerer with
her yellow eyes. "This is outrageous!" she said.
And she flung back a powerful toad–style spell.
"You're acting like a pig!" she croaked, and wished
him wallowing in some mud.
The owl disappeared, and . . .

a wild pig stomped and pawed, enraged.

This time the sorcerer didn't pause to think. With his boar brain, he snuffled angrily, ran around, tossed a chair in the air, and rumbled a belly roar. "More and more! Crash and crumble and crunch!" he growled, stamping with his hooves. His fury made him twice as strong, and three times as wild.

Meredith's poor cat saw him heading for her hiding place. With a screeching *yowl!*, she jumped for the window and sprang outside.

Then they heard a loud *splash!*

Meredith was shocked. "Are you out of your mind?
My cat has jumped into the pond!"
That's not what the sorcerer had meant to do. He
felt sorry. The two of them reversed the magic spells
so fast that lavender sparks flew out of the chimney
and a green glow seeped under the door. In an instant,
the wild pig was gone.
The sorcerer was a sorcerer again.
Meredith was Meredith.
Both of them ran from the house to save the cat.

Meredith dragged her washtub to the water's edge.
She grabbed the left oar, the sorcerer the right.
"Hold on!" cried the sorcerer to the cat.
"We're coming to save you!" called Meredith.
The cat thrashed wildly in the water until Meredith
reached her, pulled her from the water, and comforted
her with gentle words.
The sorcerer rowed them safely to shore.
"Meow!" said the cat as she jumped to land and ran
straight to a warm spot by the stove.

Meredith and the sorcerer straightened up the witch's
house. Both of them were tired.
"That's enough play for today," said the sorcerer.
"But I'll come back soon. Then we can have fun again!"
"I'd rather you didn't," said Meredith grimly.
But the sorcerer had already turned himself into a bat
and fluttered away, out the window, over the pond,
and past the tips of the trees.

It was high time for breakfast—or rather lunch.
Meredith started clanging pots and clattering pans,
and singing her cheery singing song.
The cat hissed in fright.
"Don't you worry your furry head," Meredith said.
"This time I'll watch what I say."
The two sparrows on the windowsill were
welcome guests. They sang for Meredith while she
ate, and she left them all her crumbs.